ALL MY FRIENDS

ALL
MY FRIENDS

HOPE LARSON

Farrar Straus Giroux
New York

Farrar Straus Giroux Books for Young Readers
An imprint of Macmillan Publishing Group, LLC
120 Broadway, New York, NY 10271
mackids.com

Names: Larson, Hope, author, illustrator.
Title: All my friends / Hope Larson.
Description: First edition. | New York : Farrar Straus Giroux Books for
Young Readers, 2021. | Series: [Eagle Rock] | Sequel to: All together
now. | Audience: Ages 9-14. | Audience: Grades 4-6. | Summary: When
Fancy Pink is offered a record deal their parents say no, so they decide
to make an album on their own, if they can raise enough money without
raising their parents' suspicions.
Identifiers: LCCN 2020052185 | ISBN 9780374311636 (hardcover)
ISBN 9780374388669 (trade paperback)
Subjects: LCSH: Graphic novels. | CYAC: Graphic novels. |
Musicians—Fiction. | Bands (Music)—Fiction. | Family life—California,
Southern—Fiction. | Dating (Social customs)—Fiction. | Racially mixed
people—Fiction. | California, Southern—Fiction.
Classification: LCC PZ7.7.L37 Ah 2021 | DDC 741.5/973—dc23
LC record available at https://lccn.loc.gov/2020052185

ISBN 978-0-374-31163-6 (hardcover)
1 3 5 7 9 10 8 6 4 2

ISBN 978-0-374-38866-9 (paperback)
1 3 5 7 9 10 8 6 4 2

Printed in China by Toppan Leefung Printing Ltd., Dongguan City, Guangdong Province
First edition, 2021
Book design by Hope Larson and Molly Johanson
Colored by Hilary Sycamore and Karina Edwards

March

3

You need to turn it down. I could hear you all the way at the end of the block.

Really? How'd the bass sound? I just got a vintage distortion pedal, and—

Sorry, Mom. It won't happen again.

Yeah, sorry. We just—we're excited for our show.

Right. When is it, again?

Next week at the Echo! It's, like, a really big deal.

Not *that* big. We're just the opening band.

Mm. Well. Baby steps.

click

5

One bag of gummies later . . .

Let's end practice early.

I'm not in the mood to keep playing.

munch

rustle

But we haven't practiced the new stuff!

And I'm still deciding which pedal to use!

Playing the Echo's my ultimate dream, and we're **so close** to being ready.

A few more run-throughs and we'll have it locked down. Okay? **Please?**

C'mon, Kes. What do you say?

Well . . .

Yup. Um—I'm here with Charlie. Just needed napkins.

Charlie, Austin's sister

Oh. Cool. I'm here with my dad.

Well, later!

Bye!

Got your ketchup.

Thanks! So, you and Austin are friends again?

Ew, Dad, don't spy on me!

I wasn't. I just—

We're not friends, but we're not NOT friends. Okay? It's complicated.*

*It's complicated.

They were best friends!

Until Austin got a girlfriend and started acting weird.

So Bina made new friends.

Then Austin got dumped, and Bina accidentally went on a kind-of date with him.

awkward

She couldn't figure out if she liked him or not, and ended up dumping him on their first official date.

And now things are weird.

Don't worry. It'll be okay.

I hope so.

Monday

Mt. Royal Middle School

It was **sooo** awkward, Darcy!

He came over like he wanted to talk, and then it was like he had to get away ASAP.

SLAM

I mean . . . You dumped him on your first date. He's probably not over it yet.

12

13

DOORS ARE OPEN!

Here we go!

Oh God. I invited my entire friends list. What if they don't come?

What if they all come?!

huh
huh
huh

Uh-oh. Bina, did you bring—?

A paper bag? Yep. Here ya go.

huh huh huh huh huh

Deep breaths. Yoga breaths.

In—one, two, three. Out—one, two, three.

I'll be fine—huh—when we're on—huh—stage—

Yeah, you will! We've practiced. We're ready.

We're opening for freaking Anne Surly, and we earned it.

I've been waiting all my life to stand on that stage and say—

21

The headliners

and entourage

And her parents are never home.

So we're walking around, looking at her stuff, and we end up in this giant closet.

Ooh, really?

Then what?

Everything still has the tags on. It's all stuff these **brands** sent her. So, Noah's like—

Y-you're Cooper! From Anne Surly! We **love** you!

We're Fancy Pink?

We opened for you?

...

Sorry, someone **interrupted**. What was I saying?

"So, Noah's like . . ."

dir

quotes

Right. He's like, "I bet she doesn't even know what she's got in here. We should—"

Take something?!

Leave something.

So he left his crappy old T-shirt full of sweat holes.

And two days later, Influencer Chick was wearing it on Filtergram.

Ha-ha-ha! OMG!

Let's go.

Yeah. It's **stuffy** in here.

They didn't see us play, so there's that, at least . . .

Those snobs! How **dare** they skip our set!

Even if it **was** the worst.

Cooper acts like we're dumb kids, but he's only fifteen!

Really? He seems older.

He's not! My friend goes to his school.

Hey! Fancy Pink! C'mere!

Bring a second guitar next time.

That'll give you a backup if you break another string.

Wow, great tip! I'll head straight out and buy another electric with the zillions of dollars I have lying around.

Licensing? (Inbox ✕)

 StephMerch
to: Fancy Pink
cc: Foster Levin

Dear Bina, Kesi, and Lora,

We met at the Echo. I was doing Anne Surly's merch. I checked out your EP, and it's GREAT. Can I be your #1 fan?

I'm writing because my dad works at Hala (the streaming network), and he's a fan too. He wants to know if you ever license your tracks. Specifically for this show Hala's remaking called *British Teen Private Eye*. If you're interested, he's copied here, and his name is Foster Levin.

(Don't worry, he'll understand if you're too cool to work for The Man.)

Your fan,
Steph

Okay . . .

And Bina, your share of any money you get from this deal is going into a trust, for college.

Mom! Dad! This is my big break!

Don't be such killjoys!

Aw, honey. I promise we're excited.

But you're 14! We don't want anyone taking advantage of you.

I know, but **please** don't take this chance away from me. It could change my whole life.

April

One month, 15 e-mails, 275 texts, countless parental misgivings, and a fancy grown-up meeting later . . .

Lora's house

Everybody ready?

They better not have messed with our levels. I mixed them **perfectly.**

They paid us $3,000. I think they're allowed.

Okay, well— here we go!

ZAP

Wooooo!

Seriously, if they changed **anything—**

Shhh, Lora!

hala

The original was called **British Teen Private Eye,** but—

L.A. Teen
PRIVATE EYE

We knooow, Bina!

I used to be a normal LA girl. I used to be Fun. We totally would've got along.

But when they Found a body on the Football Field, I knew it was up to me to bring **justice** to Dahlia High.

Is that—?

"Teach me a few things"?! Ew!

Thanks, but I'm busy with Fancy Pink.

Come on. Me and Todd have been playing music since sixth grade and we can't catch a break. If we had a girl in the band, we definitely would.

Yeah. People give girls way more opportunities. You don't even have to try.

I try. I started learning guitar when I was nine.

Really? Doesn't show at all.

I hope Hala paid you a lot, 'cause you need singing lessons too.

Ignore them, Bina. They're just insecure.

WILL YOU ALL STOP TELLING ME WHAT TO DO?!

Yikes. She scary.

Watch out, Austin.

Sliiiiiink

I was just trying to help.

I know. You were standing up for me, and I—

I'm sorry I yelled at you.

Hey— want to hang out later and catch up?

Yeah, maybe. Come by after school, I guess.

Cool! See you later!

Hi, Bina.

Hi, Charlie! Is Austin home?

Um, yeah.

So can I come in?

No. He isn't ready to be friends. He sent me out to intercept you.

But he said I should come over.

He said you "put him on the spot" and he "needs time to think."

If it were up to me, I'd lock you both in a room and make you talk things out. But it's not.

Oh.

Okay.

I understand.

We've been discussing the whole record label thing.

You have?

Ba DUM Ba DUM

We didn't come to this decision lightly, but . . .

Our answer is no.

What? I . . . I don't understand.

Gigging around town is one thing, but record deals are serious.

This one decision could control your life for years.

You're too young to be caught in the entertainment-industrial complex.

It's not healthy for—well—anyone, but especially not for a teenager.

51

Echo Park, Los Angeles

Saturday

Our parents are being such jerks!

I'm glad it's not just mine who're being strict.

I yelled at mine. They made me write an apology letter before I left the house.

We were about to go next level, and they just took it away.

Why don't they get what a big deal this is?

'Cause they're old.

I'm getting a refill.

Bina! Get me another croissant. I'll pay you back!

Okay—

Watch it!

Oops! Sorry!

No big. Saved by my Feline reflexes.

Hey. Don't I know you?

!!

Yeah. From the Echo greenroom.

You were mean to my band. Remember?

Oh crap. You're, uh . . .

Fancy Nancy?

Fancy Pink. Remember it. You'll be seeing a lot of us.

Um. Whoa.

What?

Speak of the devil and he shall text.

???

Hey, Steph (merch) sent me your tracks. They're great. Sorry we got off on the wrong foot.

Anyway, Anne Surly is recording an EP at Red Cent Studios and your voice is perfect for a guest vocal. Interested?

(This is Cooper from the coffee shop.)

Text Message

That's not an apology! He's not taking responsibility.

Yeah. Gross.

But it's a cool opportunity. You should do it.

I don't know. One, he's a jerk.

Two, I don't think my parents would let me.

So? Don't tell them. We'll cover for you!

Why are you so desperate for me to do this?

'Cause you'll get to learn how recording works.

The only thing really stopping us from recording our own album is, we don't know how.

Yeah! Who needs a record label? Who needs parental permission?

"No, Kesi." "Turn it down, Kesi." I'm over it!

Let's make a record ourselves!

So, Bee, what do you think?

Okay. I'll tell him I'm in.

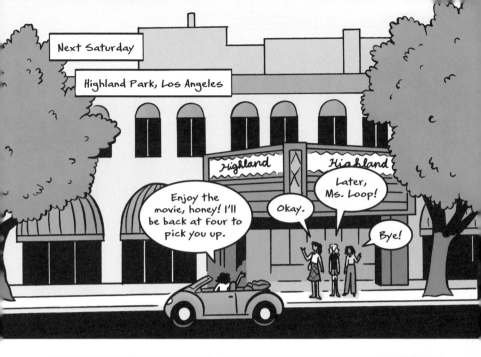

Next Saturday

Highland Park, Los Angeles

Enjoy the movie, honey! I'll be back at four to pick you up.

Okay.

Later, Ms. Loop!

Bye!

VROOM!

Do you think your parents suspect . . . ?

No, but I mean, we're barely talking right now.

There's a good taco truck around here.

No time for tacos, Lora! Come on. The studio's this way.

This is so exciting! Do you feel ready?

Yeah, mostly! I've been practicing with the demo Cooper sent me.

Red Cent Studios

You're sure this is it? What if he's messing with us?

It's the address he gave me.

Bina!

. . . and entourage.

You remember my bandmates, Lora and Kesi.

Of course!*

*Nope.

It's a tight space, and the engineer's kinda touchy, but, hey . . .

Like, how they recorded you in the bathroom?

So punk rock!

Right?!

It's official. We can for sure make a record.

All we do is show up, and the engineer makes us sound good. Easy!

We should start thinking of names for our label! How about—

Hold up. How much will all this cost?

The practical one

Oh . . .

No clue.

I could ask Cooper what he's spending.

His band has a record deal, though. They aren't the ones paying.

What about—

Bina, doesn't your friend's mom work with bands?

Yeah, Austin's mom. But she might tell my parents, so that's out.

Okay, then . . . Remember Fred from GBGB? Let's ask him.

Ugh. No. He'll want to be involved, or take credit, or—

Wait! I know someone! It's a long shot, but . . .

Ooooh, who is it?

BANK HOLIDAY

NOW SHOW...

Um, Bee? Your mom's waving to us.

Highland

Eek! We're back just in time.

Dear Gaia,

You won't remember me, but I was at your LA show. You gave me your record and told me to start a band.

I don't have a turntable yet, but I did start a band. Actually, two bands, since the first one didn't work out. The second one did, but we need some help.

A label wanted to sign us, but our parents said we're too young, so we decided to make a record ourselves. We aren't sure how to start, though, or how much it will cost. (Eeeeek.)

I know you're really busy, but if you have any advice, please write me back.

Your fan,
Bina Loop

Somewhere in Oakland, CA

Nguyen! I'm going on break!

ding

a band. n't work e help.

Hi Bina!

Glad you started a band. Love that you're sticking it to The Man. I'm happy to help you DIY your album.

First, the bad news: recording and mastering aren't cheap. If you're doing it in a studio, not on a laptop in your bedroom, the least you can realistically spend is—

Tuesday afternoon

Kesi's house

PHOO

$2,500.

And that's if we do it cheap and call in favors.

We're never going to raise that much! I'm not even allowed to get a job till next year.

I have some money saved, but my mom monitors my checking account.

If I take anything out, she'll know.

I babysit, but I'd need years to save up.

What's annoying is we'd have enough if our parents let us use the money from *LA Teen Private Eye*.

My big sister might loan us something.

I'm an only. But don't you have brothers, Bina? Can they help?

Hmm. My brother Johnny lives in Berkeley and has a husband and a cute baby and he makes bank.

He might loan us something.

I can't just call him and ask for two thousand dollars . . .

But I've got a plan.

Silence

chew chew

slurp

Mom, Dad—

She speaks!

Um, spring break is soon, and I was wondering—

Here we go. What now?

I haven't even asked yet!

You're right. I'm sorry. What is it?

Bina's Plan, Step One: Go to Berkeley

Can I go to Berkeley and visit Johnny?

Dad and I have to work.

I've flown by myself before. I want to see Johnny and Deon and the baby.

I miss them. I want to be a good aunt.

That's not a bad idea!

Hm.

Things have been tense around here. We could all stand to take a break and hit the reset button.

So, can I go?

Please?

—and while I'm there, I'll get him to loan me some money,* and then Fancy Pink can make an album!

*Not sure how, but that's a problem for Future Bina.

You're unstoppable. I've never met a girl as ambitious as me.

Go on.

You sound great on the new song. Did I tell you we finished the mix?

When can I hear it?!

Well, I was thinking, we could get ice cream and I'd play it for you, and we'd, um . . .

Get to know each other.

Wait.

Stop.

Is this, like, a date?

Do you want it to be?

Is it?

...

Oh, man—this was a mistake. You're not interested. Pretend I never opened my big dumb—

COOPER! Stop!

Let's go on a date.

Wait. Really?

Yeah. But no pressure, right? If it doesn't work out, we can still be friends?

Definitely. I promise.

No pressure at all.

Plink
Plink
Plink

Bina?

Uh-huh?

Dinner in ten.

Okay.

Um—can I please get ice cream with my friend after school on Friday?

We want to try the new place on Colorado. I can walk there from school.

Sure, honey.

Ugh. I hate this. I'm lying about everything.

Mom, wait—

It's a guy. My friend. He asked me on a date. Can I still go?

Oh.

How old is he?

Um . . . Fifteen.

My band opened for his band.

Thanks for being honest with me.

Aaand that's a no.

You can go. For one hour.

But I'll be working at the coffee shop next door, and you'll come meet me right after.

No way! I can't believe it!

Thanks, Mom! You're the best.

The date

softboy SOFT SERVE

OPEN

This feels so different from my "date" with Austin.

Thanks.

Uh-huh.

There isn't so much pressure. We haven't been friends for years. We barely know each other.

When do you leave for SF?

Berkeley. I'm going up tomorrow afternoon.

Cool.

awkward SILENCE

Do you always date girls in bands?

Fair. But you have to be a little self-obsessed so you don't give up. Right?

As a musician, I mean.

Did . . . did I say something wrong?

Sorry—I was listening. I like this band.

SCRITCH

Oh, Swearin'? Me too! This place has good music.

Did you know Allison Crutchfield lives around here?

Yeah! I follow her on Filtergram. I wish we were friends.

If you like her, you're going to love—

blah blah blah blah blah blah blah blah blah blah blah blah blah blah blah bl blah

Maybe. My perspective on that stuff changed when I became a parent.

Bina's Plan, Step Two: Ask For $$$

Oh.

Argh! I should've thought this through.

There's no way he'll lend me the money.

You're more of a rebel than I was at your age. I was always afraid to get in trouble.

Unless . . .

Do you ever wish you had?

Yeah. Sometimes.

Does that mean you'd help me get in trouble?

What exactly do you have in mind?

May

Friday afternoon

Lora's house

First order of business: Fundraising!

How much have y'all got?

Ahem—

You know how sometimes you put on an old coat, and you check the pockets, and—

How about you, Lora? Did you score big digging through couch cushions?

Twenty bucks. Wow.

"It's okay"? How come you're so chill? It's not like you.

I've been running worst-case scenarios for weeks—thank you, anxiety—and I have a backup plan.

You do?

Two words.

Benefit.

Show.

FOOM FOOM

We'll play, we'll get our friends to play, and we'll put the money from the door toward our album.

I bet Darcy and Enzo would be down.

And Anne Surly **has** to play, right? Since you're dating Cooper?

They'll bring a crowd for sure!

Um— I'll ask him.

Awww, she's blushing!

You liiiiike him!

I . . . I do. We have lots in common, and I kinda tricked him into thinking I'm cool.

I wanna date a cute band guy. Hey, is Anne Surly's drummer single?

Ignore her, Bina. When are you seeing Cooper again?

They're to thank you for letting Bina come with us.

What a lovely gesture!

Look out for this one, Jason. She can be trouble.

Mom!

No problem. Got my peepers lasered last year.

Ready, kids?

Yes, sir.

Yeah!

Be good!

Okaaaay!

Fred! Hey!

Huh?
Oh, Bina!

Fred, booker/promoter at all-ages DIY space GBGB

Sup, girl? Excited for Buy Generic?

I don't really know them. I came with Cooper.

Hold up. The frontwoman of Fancy Pink and the frontman of Anne Surly . . . ?

Anything within my power.

Calm down. It's only our second date.

Anyway.

I was hoping you could do me a giant favor.

So, Kesi and Lora and I are doing a benefit show to cover our recording costs—

Rad! I'll be there.

Aaactually, I was hoping you'd give us the room at GBGB for, like . . . free?

Oh . . .

Er . . .

No? Okay. I know it's a lot to ask.

It's not that . . .

What?! But why?

There's no more GBGB. The city shut us down.

There was a Fire at a warehouse party up in Oakland. Total nightmare. People **died**.

The city doesn't want the same thing happening here, so they're shutting down alternative spaces, and GBGB got caught in the net.

That sucks, Fred. I'm sorry.

I'll find another spot, but for now . . .

Sorry I can't help.

It's okay. I know you would if you could.

Lemme know where you land! I'll help get the word out.

I will! Thanks, Fred!

119

It's okay.

Really?

I wasn't feeling the chemistry either.

Phew. The music scene's just so small, and I don't want things to be awkward, and—

Oh! Will you still play Fancy Pink's benefit?

Of course! You're going places.

I'd be stupid not to come along.

Let's hang out soon. As friends.

Compatriots in music.

Yeah. Definitely.

"Everything's Fine."

SPLISH

CLUNK CLUNK

Oof.

Austin gets me. And I get him.

Mustard-grilled patties are gross, but I like that he orders them that way.

And it's not just burger orders— it's everything. Why didn't I realize how special that is?

126

That wasn't too weird.

Standing next to him didn't make me feel, like, **crazed** or anything.

I like him, I like him not. I like him, I like him not. I like him—

Um? You're in my seat?

Wha?

Aren't you in, like, eighth grade?

Huh?

Kesi's house

It's cool we're getting a room for free, Bina, but I wish we didn't have to do a daytime show.

FANCY PINK

RAT-A-TAT

Are you kidding? A daytime Saturday show is perfect!

Street fruit salad

One, our parents won't suspect anything.

TA TAT TA TAT TA

Two, our friends with curfews will get to come.

TAT TA
TA TAT
TA
TAT

Three, would you please stop drumming?! You're making me anxious!

Ahem—

Sorry!

How's this look?

June

It's going to be a **disaster!**

I'm going to humiliate myself **again!**

I'm going to—

Bina! Shut up!

Just 'cause things went wrong before, it doesn't mean they will again.

PAT PAT

Sniff

I bet every one of your favorite rock stars has broken, like, a million strings.

SLUMP

Yeah . . . But they have roadies to hand them another guitar.

143

Is Austin coming? I put a Flyer in his locker, but . . .

Um . . .

I don't think so.

Oh.

I don't know if you can change his mind, but I wrote a new song.

For him.

I wrote a song for him.

No promises, okay? But I'll do my best.

I kinda doubt that's all she does.

Aw, there's no way!

I sent him my new song last night, and we texted for an hour, but he never mentioned—

I know you're friends, but it's lame that he didn't warn you.

Are you sure you're okay?

Uh . . .

I . . .

AHEM.

What's happening here?

flinch

Me and Steph? Yeah. It was, um, unexpected.

You're not upset, right? 'Cause you broke things off, so . . .

It's cool, Cooper. She's cool. I approve.

Thanks.

We're getting food after the show, and you should come if you're not—

Bina!

Hey, Kesi? Got a paper bag?

Don't need one. I'm not stressed at all!

ZIIIP

We already played our worst show ever. We've got nowhere to go but up.

dab

fluff

I wasn't asking for you, I was asking for—

171

172

173

After the show

Hey.

Austin!

Um, I—

What now? I spent all that time thinking about making the grand gesture.

I never thought about what comes after.

I like the new song.

Really? But—

But you said you only came 'cause Charlie said you should.

Lora! Feeling better?

Yeah! For real this time.

Sucks that I missed the show, but guess what?

What?

We did it!

Really?! We got the money?

WE'RE MAKING A RECORD!

181

We wanted to hear you play!

But how— how did you hear about the show?

I told them.

Charlie! You ratted Bina out?!

I did not!

Kids! Enough!

Give me a little credit, huh? It's my **job** to know when cool new bands are breaking.

Bina wallpapered the east side with flyers for a tantilizing secret show, but there aren't any secrets in this town. The folks who run Sinkhole are old friends of mine.

Those flyers worked a little too well, I guess.

So, um . . .

i ♥ u

What'd you think of our set?

Granted, we were listening from out here, but . . .

You sounded great!

We're proud of you, Bee.

I'm not in trouble?

HA HA HA HA HA

Oh, you're in huge trouble.

You'll have to hold off recording your album, because you're very, very grounded.

You're grounded?!

You didn't tell our parents, right?

We-e-e-ell . . .

HONK HONK

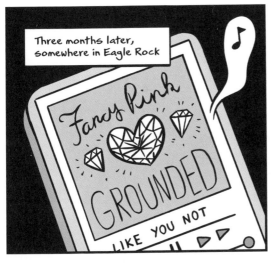

Three months later, somewhere in Eagle Rock

Fancy Pink
GROUNDED
LIKE YOU NOT

Daisy petals one, two, three

This is the best song ever.

Maybe we should start a band.

Yeah.

Definitely.

Meanwhile, a few blocks away

The End